CORIANDER

THE CONTRARY HEN

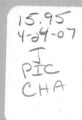
For Stephanie—my pride and joy
—D.C.

For my wonderful friend Sue,
and forever Mush and Poot.
Special thanks to McNevin.
—M.G.C.

Carolrhoda Books, Inc.
A division of Lerner Publishing Group
241 First Avenue North
Minneapolis, MN 55401 U.S.A.

Website address: www.lernerbooks.com

Library of Congress Cataloging-in-Publication Data
Chaconas, Dori, 1938–
      Coriander the contrary hen by Dori Chaconas ; illustrations
by Marsha Gray Carrington.
          p. cm.
      Summary: Coriander the contrary hen sits refusing to move in
the middle of the road, causing a traffic jam until one clever little
girl comes up with a solution.
          ISBN-13: 978-1-57505-749-1 (lib. bdg. : alk. paper)
          ISBN-10: 1-57505-749-2 (lib. bdg. : alk. paper)
          1 Chickens—Fiction.   2. Domestic animals—Fiction.
3. Farm life—Fiction.   I. Carrington, Marsha Gray, ill.   II. Title.
    PZ7.C342Cnn 2007
    [E]—dc22   2005015004

Manufactured in the United States of America
1 2 3 4 5 6 – DP – 12 11 10 09 08 07

CORIANDER THE CONTRARY HEN

DORI CHACONAS   Illustrated by **MARSHA GRAY CARRINGTON**

CAROLRHODA BOOKS, INC. MINNEAPOLIS • NEW YORK

Coriander was a contrary hen.

When Farmer Bucket said, "Go!"
Coriander stayed.

When Mrs. Bucket said, "Stay!"
Coriander got up and went.

When little Fanny Bucket told Coriander not to dig in the garden, Coriander dug up three pea plants and ate half a row of baby lettuce.

One day, all the chickens settled their ruffled bottoms in the henhouse. But Coriander, the contrary hen, didn't want to settle her ruffled bottom in the henhouse.

So she scratched her way under the henhouse fence. She marched through the tall grass. She pulled out some grass with her beak and piled it in the middle of the road.

Then she sat . . .
and sat . . .
and sat.

Rumble-GRUMBLE! Skreeeck!

A pig truck slid to a stop, a hair's width away from Coriander. Farmer Bucket came running.

"Coriander!" Farmer Bucket said.
"You can't sit in the middle of the road!
This road is not for hens!
This road is for trucks!"

With a ruffle of her feathers
and a sharp look in her eye,
Coriander cackled
a discourteous reply,

CLUCK CLUCK TRUCK!

"Don't sass me!" Farmer Bucket said. "Get back to the henhouse!"

But Coriander just shook her head and gave Farmer Bucket a peck on his boot. She tucked her grass nest deeper into the road.

Then she sat . . .
  and sat . . .
    and sat.

"Clear the road!" the truck driver called. "Move your hen!"

Chuggle-shuggle! Skreeeck!

A tractor slid to a stop, a hair's width away
from the pig truck.

Mrs. Bucket ran up from the well with her
water pail sloshing.

"**Coriander!**" Mrs. Bucket said. "You can't sit in the middle of the road! You're blocking the traffic. And what if it rains? You and your nest will get stuck in the muck!"

With a ruffle of her feathers and a sharp look in her eye, Coriander cackled a discourteous reply,

CLUCK CLUCK MUCK!

"Don't be flippant with me!" said Mrs. Bucket. "Get back to the henhouse!"

But Coriander just ruffled her feathers and gave Mrs. Bucket a peck on her water pail. She flattened herself deeper into the road.

Then she sat . . .
 and sat . . .
  and sat.

"We can't get through!" the tractor driver called. "Move your hen!"

Honk-a-honk! Skreeeck!

A school bus slid to a stop, a hair's width away from the tractor.

Little Fanny Bucket hopped off the bus.

"Coriander Hen!"

she scolded. "You can **NOT** sit in the middle of the road! You are not acting like a smart hen. You're acting like a dumb duck!"

With a ruffle of her feathers and a sharp look in her eye, Coriander cackled a discourteous reply,

CLUCK CLUCK DUCK!

Fanny squinted at Coriander with one eye.
Then she shook her finger at the hen.
"That's not funny!" she said.
"Go back to the henhouse!"

But Coriander, the
contrary hen, just squinted
back with one eye and shook
her wing feathers at
Fanny. She gave Fanny
a peck on her
schoolbag.
She scratched
herself deeper
into the road.

Then she sat . . . and sat . . . and sat.

Three more trucks, two hay wagons, one cement mixer,
and six automobiles stopped behind the school bus.

The driver in the pig truck shouted, "MOVE YOUR HEN!"

The driver on the tractor shouted, "MOVE YOUR HEN!"

The children on the school bus shouted, "MOVE YOUR DUMB DUCK!"

Every driver in every vehicle shouted,

"MOVE YOUR HEN!"

But Coriander just sat . . .

and sat . . .

and sat.

"We have a real problem here," Farmer Bucket said.

"What are we going to do?" asked Mrs. Bucket.

"One of us is going to have to move her,"
said little Fanny Bucket.

"Not me!" Farmer Bucket answered.
"Look at that pointy beak! I could
get a bad peck on the head if I
tried to move that contrary hen."

"And not me!" Mrs. Bucket said.
"Look at those sharp toenails! I
could get a bad scratch on the nose
if I tried to move that contrary hen!"

"Enough!" Fanny yelled.
"I'll do it myself! You just
need to be a little bit
smarter than a contrary hen."

Fanny changed her face from sour to sweet, then walked right up to Coriander.

"Coriander," Fanny Bucket said, sweet as honey. "Just never you mind this tangled-up traffic jam. You just stay right there. Do you hear me, Coriander? Do **NOT** get out of the road. Do **NOT** go back to the henhouse. And most importantly, do **NOT** do what anyone asks you to do!"

Coriander, the contrary hen,
looked Fanny Bucket
straight in the eye.

She flicked her tail feathers.

She stuck her beak in the air.

She stood up and kicked
the grass nest.

Then Coriander marched
straight to the henhouse.

"You did it!" Mrs. Bucket said to Fanny.
"Smart thinking!" Farmer Bucket agreed.

Coriander looked at all the other nests.
"Cluck!" warned all the other hens.

The best nests were taken.

At the end of the row sat the very last nest.
It was scruffy. It was lined with only
a few wisps of scratchy straw.

But once a contrary hen,
always a contrary hen . . .

Coriander looked at all the feathers
on the ruffled bottoms of the hens.
And with a ruffle of her feathers
and a sharp look in her eye,
Coriander cackled a discourteous reply,